P9-CQE-786

For Suzanne

PHILOMEL BOOKS
A division of Penguin Young Readers Group.
Published by The Penguin Group.

Penguin Group (USA) Inc., 375 Hudson Street, New York, NY 10014, U.S.A.
Penguin Group (Canada), 90 Eglinton Avenue East, Suite 700, Toronto, Ontario M4P 2Y3, Canada (a division of Pearson Penguin Canada Inc.).
Penguin Books Ltd, 80 Strand, London WC2R 0RL, England.
Penguin Ireland, 25 St. Stephen's Green, Dublin 2, Ireland (a division of Penguin Books Ltd).
Penguin Group (Australia), 250 Camberwell Road, Camberwell, Victoria 3124, Australia (a division of Pearson Australia Group Pty Ltd).
Penguin Books India Pvt Ltd, 11 Community Centre, Panchsheel Park, New Delhi – 110 017, India.
Penguin Group (NZ), 67 Apollo Drive, Rosedale, North Shore 0632, New Zealand (a division of Pearson New Zealand Ltd).
Penguin Books (South Africa) (Pty) Ltd, 24 Sturdee Avenue, Rosebank, Johannesburg 2196, South Africa.
Penguin Books Ltd, Registered Offices: 80 Strand, London WC2R 0RL, England.

Library of Congress Cataloging-in-Publication Data available upon request.
ISBN 978-0-399-25074-3
3 5 7 9 10 8 6 4

The Way Back Home

Oliver Jeffers

PHILOMEL BOOKS

Once there was a boy,

and one day, as he was putting
his things back in the closet,
he found an airplane.

He didn't remember leaving it in there, but
he thought he'd take it out for a go right away.

The plane lifted off the ground
and up into the sky . . .

higher   and higher   and higher.

Suddenly the plane sputtered . . .

p hut

phut

PHut

It had run out of fuel.

Now the boy was stuck on the moon.

What was he to do?

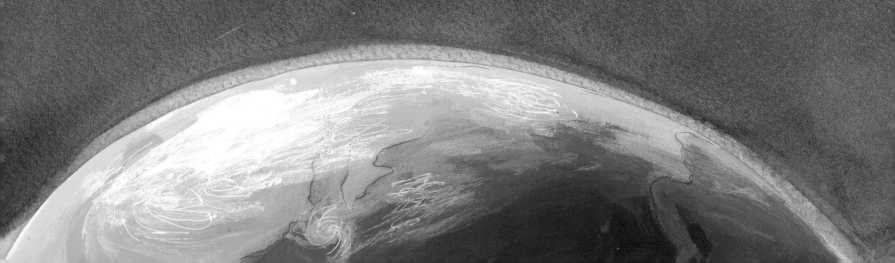

He was all alone and afraid
and soon his flashlight began to go out.

Meanwhile, up in space
someone else was in trouble too.

His engine
had broken down . . .

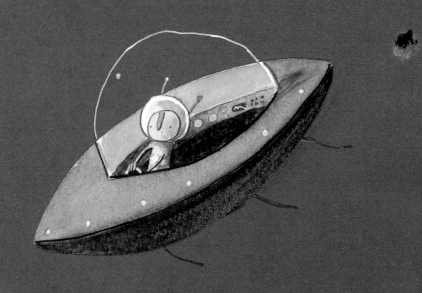

and steering the ship
toward a flicker of light,
he landed on the moon
with a bump.

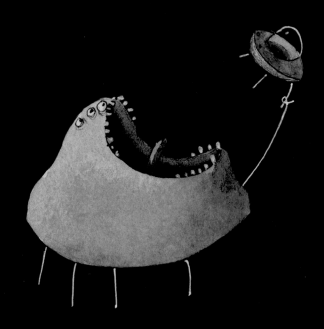

The boy heard noises.
The Martian heard noises.
Both feared the worst.

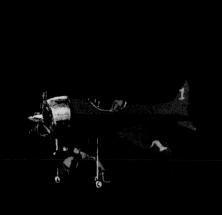
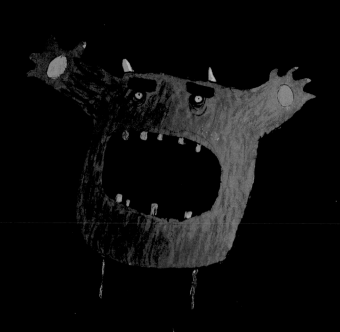

But as their eyes
got used to the dark,
both the boy and
the Martian realized
they'd met someone else
in trouble.

They weren't
alone anymore.

The boy showed the Martian his empty fuel tank
and the Martian showed the boy his broken engine.

Together they thought of ways to fix their machines
and get them both back home.

As the earth was nearest,
the boy went first.
Down he jumped . . .

right

into

the

sea . . .

and *swam* toward home.

But by the time he got there, the boy
was tired out, so he sat in his favorite chair,
just to catch his breath.

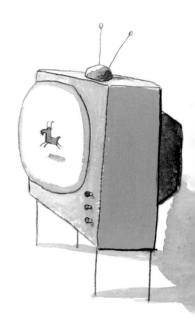

His favorite
program was just starting,
and he settled down to watch.

Suddenly he remembered
what he should be doing!
He rushed off to the closet
to get what he needed.
Then he ran outside and shouted.
But there was no reply.
He couldn't be heard.

The boy
climbed to
higher ground,
called again,
and waited.

This time,
a rope was lowered.

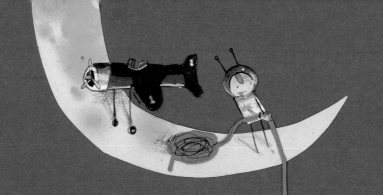

The boy
began to climb
and the Martian
began to pull,
and soon the
boy was back
on the moon.

The boy fixed up the Martian's ship
with a couple of rubber bands and a wrench
while the Martian filled the boy's fuel tank.

They said good-bye and
thanked each other for their help.

They wondered if
they'd ever meet again.

After a long and tiring night,
they were both finally
off the moon.

The boy went one way and
the Martian went another,
both on their way back home.

hello?
hello?